THE FLINTSTONES
THE MYSTERY OF
MAMMOTH MANSION

Copyright © 1978 Hanna-Barbera Productions, Inc.
Published by Ottenheimer Publishers, Inc.
Printed in U.S.A. All Rights Reserved.
Published simultaneously in Canada.

"Taking the Bedrock book census is going to be a soft job," said Fred Flintstone to his friend, Barney Rubble, as the two men walked down the street. "We've already counted three libraries and there's only one more to go before our work is over for the day."

"Where do we have to go next?" asked Barney.

Fred looked at a piece of paper that was attached to the clipboard he was carrying.

"It says on the list, that we have to go to Mammoth Mansion," answered Fred, pointing at a huge house that looked down at them menacingly from the top of the large, barren hill they were approaching.

Barney shuddered. "I don't know, Fred," he said. "I've heard some strange rumors about that place. They say no one will live there because strange things happen."

"Don't tell me you believe in ghosts, Barney," said Fred. "You're a grown man."

Fred and Barney climbed the front porch steps of Mammoth

Mansion and Fred stopped to check his clipboard again.

"I have a note here that says we can just go in. The owner knew we would be coming so he left the door unlocked."

"I still don't like it, Fred. This place gives me the creeps," said Barney.

Fred just laughed. He grasped the ornate knob of the front door and pushed. The door opened easily.

Inside, the only light in the front hall was the sunlight which came through the large front windows. The floor was bare and there were objects, shrouded in white sheets, scattered across it. A large and winding staircase loomed invitingly in front of Fred and Barney.

"We may as well get started," said Fred, enthusiastically, and without hesitation, he began to ascend the stairs. Barney shook his head doubtfully, but he followed Fred.

When they reached the top of the staircase, they saw a thick wooden door with an elaborately lettered sign on it that said, **Library.** Fred opened the door, and he and Barney peered cautiously into the library. The room smelled of old age and disuse. Dust, in thick layers, covered everything. The walls of the library were lined with massive bookshelves, which touched the ceiling. Every shelf was filled with books of various sizes, bound in earth-toned leather.

"Do you think we should go in

here, Fred?" asked Barney.

"Don't be silly," Fred replied. "It's our job." The two men walked slowly into the room. The wood floor creaked and groaned as they walked across it. Behind them, the door closed silently by itself.

"Where do we start?" asked Barney.

"You start at one side of the door, and I'll start at the other," said Fred. "We'll meet at the window."

Fred busied himself, counting the books under his breath, and Barney hastened to follow his example. Before long, however, Barney found himself distracted by the rows of inviting books. There were volumes on every subject imaginable and the huge bookshelves seemed to

stare down at him, urging him to pick one. Barney stopped counting and began to read the titles to himself, becoming hypnotized by the promise of all the many adventures offered to him in the books. As if it had a will of its own, his arm reached out, and took down a large book, expensively bound in dark brown leather.

"Stories Of The Old West," he read to himself. Instantly, his mind was bombarded by images of wide open plains, marauding Indians, and hard-faced outlaws. The speed at which the pictures flashed through his mind was astounding, and Barney, unable to control them, became dizzy. He lost his balance and had to lean against the bookshelf for

support. He shook his head to clear it and the images went away. He was left with a strange empty feeling, however; as if he had been left behind when everyone else had gone for a picnic. He remembered the book, which he still held tightly in his hand, and without a moment's hesitation, he opened it and began reading the first page. Suddenly, as if from far away, he heard Fred's voice calling to him. The sound annoyed him and he tried to ignore it, but it would not go away. Then he felt himself being shaken violently by something or someone that he could not see clearly. This intrusion into his dream world startled Barney and the book accidentally fell from his hands.

All of a sudden, the worried and frightened face of Fred Flintstone popped into view right in front of him. The details of the room snapped into focus abruptly, and Barney felt a momentary disorientation.

"Barney! Barney!" shouted Fred, "are you all right? Speak to me!"

"What's the matter, Fred?" asked Barney. "You look like you've just seen a ghost!"

"I just did," cried Fred. "I looked over to see how you were doing and I could see right through you! It scared me silly!"

"That's ridiculous, Fred," said Barney. "I've been right here counting the books like you told me. I stopped just now because I was feeling a little dizzy, but

that's just from craning my neck to see the top shelves."

"Barney, I tell you, I saw you fading away," said Fred. "Look, let's finish this job as fast as we can. This whole house is beginning to give me the creeps, too."

"If you say so," said Barney, shaking his head, "but I think you should go see a doctor and get your eyes checked, Fred."

The two men walked over to the door and Fred grasped the ornate knob and pulled. The door refused to budge.

"It's stuck," Fred said, disgustedly. Bracing himself, Fred put both hands on the knob and pulled as hard as he could. The door still would not open.

"Help me, Barney," he grunted, and the two men pulled together with all of their strength. It was no use.

"Did you lock the door when we came in?" asked Barney.

"There's no lock on this door," said Fred pointing to the knob. "I don't understand it! We will ju ....! Fred stopped speaking abruptly as he quickly realized, with horror, that his friend, Barney, was no longer listening. Oblivious to everything else, Barney turned and began walking slowly back to the bookshelves, a vacant look on his face. He then stooped mechanically and picked up the book which he had dropped a few minutes before. As he began

to open the book, Fred hurried up to him and tried to grab it away.

"Barney, this is no time to read a book," he said.

Barney refused to let go, however, and in spite of Fred's tugging, he began to read the book out loud. Instantly, the room became fuzzy and a moment later, it began to fade.

"Barney!" cried Fred. "What's happening?"

But Barney would not answer. Instead, he continued to read, and with each word, the library became less and less distinct. When the room had almost faded entirely, new images began to appear. Fred let go of the book with one hand and rubbed his eyes in an effort to

make sense of the confusing overlay of the images. He thought he saw cactus and miles and miles of rolling hills and sand, but his mind refused to accept the fact that these things were in the library of Mammoth Mansion. Then, the library disappeared! With startling suddenness, Fred found himself and Barney standing in the middle of the desert with no evidence of civilization in sight. For miles in every direction, there was nothing but rocky ground, sagebrush, and cactus. The sun, high overhead, beat down unmercifully.

At that moment, Barney stopped reading. He came out of the trance suddenly and as he looked around, trying to clear his

mind, Fred could see that his friend was disturbed and frightened.

"Wh-wh-where are we, Fred?" he asked, his voice on the edge of hysteria. "This isn't the library!"

"No, Barney," Fred replied, "it certainly isn't! You brought us here somehow, when you read that book."

Barney looked down at the book that he still held in his hands as if he had never seen it before. "I don't remember reading a book," he said in disbelief.

"Well, whether you remember or don't remember, it's not important now," said Fred. "What **is** important is that we get out of this sun and find ourselves some shade. I'm thirsty, too."

"What do I do with this?" asked Barney, holding up the book.

"You'd better keep it just in case we need it," Fred answered. "It brought us here, and I have a feeling it's the key to returning to the library."

Barney opened the book again, and began to read. After a few moments, he looked up at Fred in amazement.

"It says right here, on page twenty-three that Fred and his faithful sidekick, Barney, were stranded in the desert," he said.

"The book said all of that?" asked Fred.

"Yeah, and it says that they were rescued by a kind cowboy."

"Well, why don't you read on and see what happens next."

"I tried that, Fred," said Barney anxiously, "but it only goes for a short distance into the future. I tried skipping to the end, but all the pages are blank!"

"We're writing this book," said Fred in amazement. "This book is our adventure. That means we won't get out of here until it's finished and we don't even know if it's got a happy ending!"

Just then, Fred and Barney heard the rhythmic drumming of a horse's hooves on the dry ground and they looked up to see a cowboy riding toward them from out of the desert.

"Here's our cowboy, right on schedule," said Fred.

When he was a few feet away, he stopped and looked at Fred

and Barney with great interest. He was tall and thin, and he wore a big ten-gallon hat. He was dressed in high boots and a plaid shirt and he wore a colorful bandana around his neck. His legs were covered by thick chaps and he carried a coiled rope on his saddle.

"Howdy, strangers," he said, with a wide grin on his face. "It looks like you fellers are in a heap of trouble. How did you get out here? Were you held up?"

"That's a long story that I'm not sure you will believe," said Fred. "Right now, my friend and I could use a drink of water."

The cowboy frowned. "You fellers aren't cattle thieves, are you? We don't cotton to rustlers around here."

"No, we're not rustlers," Fred hastened to assure him. "We, er, went out for a walk and got lost, that's all."

The cowboy looked at them strangely for a moment, then he laughed. "I guess the sun has driven you fellers plumb loco. My name's Jim and I'm riding point for a cattle herd that's passing through these parts. You'll have to forgive my jumping to conclusions about you being rustlers, but there's been a lot of cattle thieving on this stretch of the trail. We can't seem to catch them and they're robbing us blind. They steal our cattle and then just disappear! But enough of that. I'm going to take you fellers back to camp with me. I

think you could use some rest. Hop on the back of my horse."

Fred and Barney looked at the horse with misgivings, but they climbed on. Anything was better than staying in the desert, and besides, it was written that way in the book.

A short time later, Jim's sturdy cow pony reached the top of a hill and Fred and Barney, riding behind the saddle, got their first glimpse of the huge herd of cattle grazing in the valley below.

"There's the camp," said Jim, pointing to a tiny group of wagons and tents in the middle of the valley.

"Gosh," said Fred. "I don't think I've ever seen that many of one kind of animal together at one time!"

Jim guided his horse skillfully down into the valley, threading his way through the cattle, until they reached the small camp. Jim stopped his horse in front of a large wagon that was filled with pots and pans.

"This here's the chuck wagon, boys," he explained.

"What's chuck?" asked Fred.

Jim looked at Fred and Barney in amazement. "You two guys really are dudes," he said.

"What have you brought into camp this time?" asked a short bearded man, coming up to them from around the side of the wagon. Jim laughed.

"I picked these two strays up in the desert, Cookie," he said,

indicating Fred and Barney. "Can you believe that I found them on foot without food or water?"

"They're dudes for sure," laughed Cookie. "Chuck is cowboy talk for food. Let me introduce myself," he added, bowing with mock formality. "I'm the cook. That's why they call me Cookie. You fellers look like you could use some good chow. Get on down from that horse and sit yourselves by the fire."

Fred and Barney were glad to get off the horse, but when they reached the ground, they both groaned as they tried to stand up straight. Jim laughed so hard at their plight that he almost fell off his horse.

"You're saddle sore," he

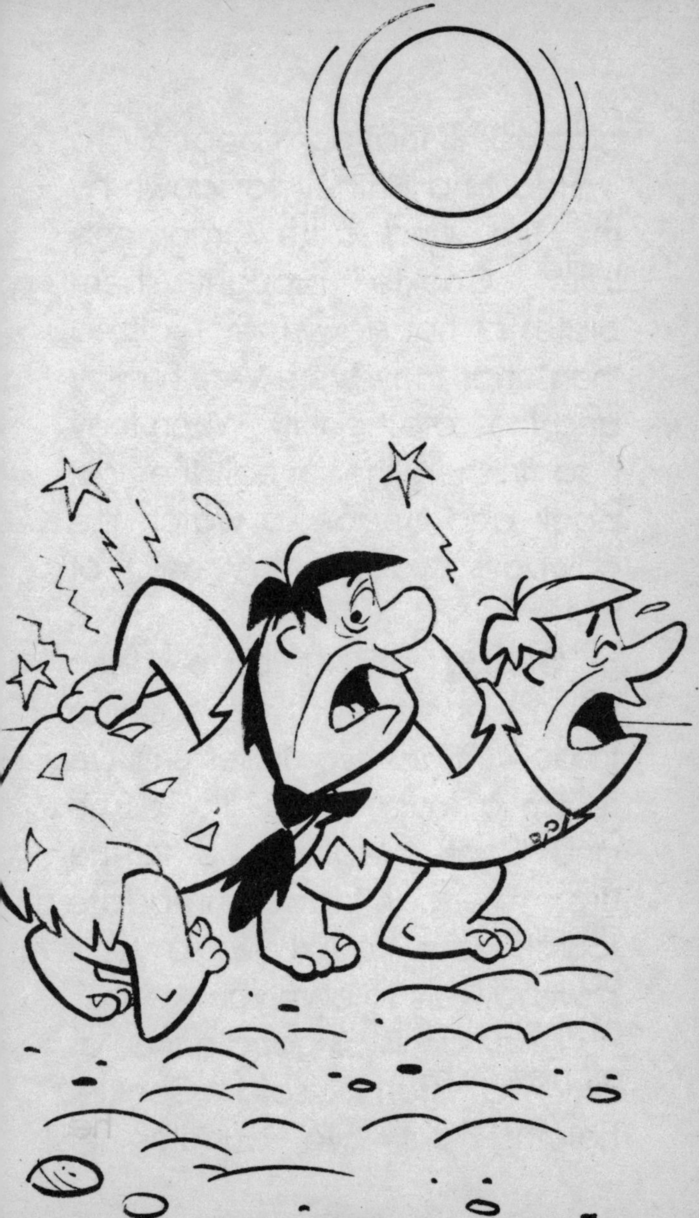

gasped. "If that don't beat all."

Fred and Barney sat down by the fire, and a few moments later, Cookie brought them plates of hot stew. They realized then, that they were very hungry and they ate heartily. When they had finished their meal, they sat back and began to watch the cowboys working the herd of cattle.

"Cookie and I have been talking about what we're going to do with you two dudes until we reach a town," said Jim, as he and Cookie walked up to the fire. "We can't accommodate tourists here, you know, so you'll have to work to earn your keep."

"And now is as good a time as any to start," said Cookie, holding out two bundles of

clothing to Fred and Barney. "I found these extra duds in the wagon. They should fit all right. Go and try them on."

Fred and Barney took the bundles and went behind the wagon. When they came out, they were dressed like Jim, in high boots, chaps, and ten-gallon hats. They had bright bandanas around their necks, and they each carried a coiled rope in their hands.

"Now I'm going to teach you how to work cattle," said Jim. "Follow me." The tall cowboy led them to the picket line, where he selected two horses and saddled them. "These two horses are gentle," he said.

Fred and Barney looked at the two horses doubtfully. They certainly didn't look gentle.

"Y-y-you go first, Fred," said Barney.

"S-s-sure, Barney," agreed Fred, trying his best to be brave.

"Quit stalling," said Jim. "I haven't got all night!"

Fred put his foot into the stirrup, as he had seen Jim do, and heaved himself into the saddle. To his relief the horse merely stood still and looked at Fred with a bored expression on its face. Fred relaxed a bit then, and he sat back in the saddle, grasping the reins in his left hand.

"That's very good," said Jim. "Now give him a little nudge in the ribs with your boots and he'll move forward. When you want him to turn to the left, pull the reins to the left. When you want him to turn right, pull the reins to the right. It's called neck reining."

Fred, feeling confident, since things had gone well with the riding lesson so far, smiled at Barney and Jim as he gave the horse a firm kick. Two bucks and a jump later, Fred found himself on the ground looking up at the horse. The animal had come over to look at Fred, and it raised its head and curled its upper lip above its teeth.

"He's laughing at you," said Jim, as he and Barney rolled on the ground with laughter.

"I'd like to see **you** try it, Barney," said Fred, angry and embarrassed.

At that, Barney stopped laughing. "I don't think I want to try it, Fred," he said seriously.

"You kicked him too hard," said Jim. "Mount up, both of you, and let's go watch the herd."

Fred, Barney and Jim rode out of the camp toward the herd of cattle, quietly grazing.

"We can sure use your help, men," Jim said to Fred and Barney, as they rode out of the camp. "We've been having a lot of trouble with cattle thieves."

"How do you steal something as big as a cattle herd?" asked Fred.

"Usually, it's done by making a lot of noise and frightening the cattle. They start to run then, and it's pretty hard to stop them. It's called stampeding the cattle. When the thieves get them running, they can herd them just about any place. The thieves

travel in large gangs and there's usually too many of them for the cowboys to fight. They take the cattle and sell them before the law can catch up to them. We have to keep watch on the cattle all of the time. The cowboys ride around the herd to keep them quiet. The cattle are comforted when they hear the cowboys talk or sing to them. That will be your job, men. You can talk to them or sing if you want. I've got to check on the other riders now. I'll be back to check on you in a little while."

Fred and Barney looked forlornly after him, as the tall cowboy rode off toward another part of the herd.

"What do you say to a bunch of cattle?" asked Barney bewildered.

"It beats me, Barney," answered Fred. He turned to the nearest cow and tipped his hat. "Hello there, Mr. Cow," he said. "How are you this evening?"

The cow stared at him stupidly, and Fred threw up his hands in disgust. "This isn't going to work," he said. "Jim said we could sing to them. The only songs I know are the ones I sing to Pebbles."

"Let's give it a try, Fred," said Barney.

"Rock-a-bye baby, on a tree top, when the wind blows, the cradle will rock," sang Fred.

"I think it's working," said Barney. "They're closing their eyes."

"I think it's working on my horse, too," said Fred. "He's sound asleep."

"This is an easy job," said Barney.

"It's also very boring," said Fred. "Get out the book, Barney, and see if it says anything about how long we're going to be doing this."

Barney took out the book and began thumbing through the pages.

"Here we are, page fifty-seven. 'The two fearless cowboys stood watch on the restless herd.' I guess that's us, Fred."

"Keep reading," urged Fred.

"Suddenly, from out of the hills,

there rode a screaming band of outlaws . . . .!"

"Outlaws!" cried Fred. "Barney, we've got to warn the cowboys! There's going to be a stampede!"

But it was too late, for just as Fred was about to find Jim to warn him, riders appeared on the horizon. They came riding down on the cattle herd from the hills surrounding the valley. They wore their bandanas over their faces like masks and as they rode, they waved blankets in the air over their heads and shouted at the cattle. The cattle became frightened and began to run, sending up great clouds of dust into the air with their hooves.

Fred's horse woke up with a start at the first sound of trouble. An experienced cow pony, it

knew immediately what was happening, and it began to run in an effort to save itself and its rider from the fear-crazed cattle. Barney's horse followed it and Fred and Barney could only hang on to their saddle horns and hope that they would not fall off and be trampled by the panicking cattle.

From somewhere behind them, Fred and Barney heard Jim shouting at them.

"We've got to try to turn the herd!" he shouted. "Slow down and let me catch up to you."

But Fred's horse had its own idea about what to do and it ignored Fred's efforts to stop it.

"Come on, horse," said Fred, trying to keep his voice calm. "Please slow down. Let's be

reasonable. You're the horse and I'm the rider. You're supposed to do what I say." The horse was not listening to Fred, however, for it kept on running with the cattle. Fred gathered up the reins in both hands and pulled back as hard as he could. The horse responded and began to slow down when, all of a sudden, the reins broke! Feeling itself free, the horse began to run even faster after the cattle. Fred grabbed the saddle horn just in time to keep from being thrown off. He now had no way to stop his horse, and he was at the mercy of the animal.

"Get ahead of me, Barney," he shouted over his shoulder. "If you can stop your horse, maybe mine will follow it!"

"I can't catch up to you," Barney yelled back. "Your horse is too fast!"

The dust in the air was getting thicker and the cattle showed no sign of slowing down. Fred put his bandana over his nose to keep from choking. Squinting through the dust, he could see that Barney and the other cowboys had done the same. Now, however, it was impossible to tell the cowboys from the cattle thieves, and everything became even more confused than before. Fred thought he recognized a few of the cowboys as they rode by him, but he wasn't sure.

At that moment, a rider whom Fred could not identify, rode up next to him. Reaching over, the man grabbed the dangling ends

of the broken reins and began leading Fred's horse away from the running herd.

"You'll be safe, now," the man shouted to Fred.

Fred glanced over his shoulder and saw that Barney's horse had turned to follow. The dust was still very thick all around them, and although he tried, Fred could not see where he was going. He knew the cattle were still running but he could not tell in what direction. The only thing he could do was hang on to the saddle horn and hope that everything would come out all right and that Jim and the other cowboys could somehow stop the stampede.

He rode on this way for some

time — how long, he could not tell — when suddenly he felt his horse begin to slow down. The cattle slowed down, too. And presently, they stopped running. The rider who had taken hold of Fred's horse, let go and rode off. Barney pulled up along side of Fred and then pulled back on the reins of his horse, commanding it to stop. Fred's horse followed its lead and stopped as well.

"That was some ride," sighed Barney, when he had caught his breath.

"Yeah," said Fred, breathing a sigh of relief. "I wonder how Jim and the boys got these cattle to stop running?"

With the cattle stopped, the dust was beginning to clear. Fred

and Barney squinted through it trying to make out their situation. What they saw made them uneasy.

The camp was nowhere to be seen. They hurriedly looked around for Jim but they could not see him and they couldn't see anyone they knew. The herd seemed smaller, too, and as they looked around, Fred realized that they were no longer in the valley.

"I don't like the looks of this," Fred said to Barney.

Just then, the rider who had led Fred's horse rode up to them. He squinted at Fred and then he stared angrily.

"I thought you were my friend Jeb," he said, "but you're just one of the cowboys! I see you've

got one of your pals with you, too. The boss ain't going to like this one bit. You'd better come with me."

The outlaw took Fred and Barney toward what seemed like an open plain with some gently rolling hills. The man stopped in front of one of the hills and gave a low whistle. To Fred's and Barney's surprise, a patch of the grass covering the hill began to move and a door appeared on the side of the hill.

"No wonder the cowboys haven't been able to catch the cattle thieves," whispered Fred to Barney. "Their hideout is inside the hill!"

A big tough looking man came out of the door and looked at Fred and Barney menacingly.

"What have you gone and dragged into camp this time, Bill?" he asked the man who had brought Fred and Barney to the hideout. "I thought I told you never to bring strangers to the hideout without my permission."

"B-B-b-b-but, Big Jake," stammered the rustler, "I couldn't help it this time. When we were stealing the cattle, my friend Jeb got lost and I mistook this cowboy for him. I seen he was in trouble and I helped him. This other feller," he added pointing to Barney, "just sort of came along."

Big Jake looked at Fred and Barney again. "It looks like I'm going to have to tie you two fellers up until I decide what to do with you. Get them down, Bill, and take them inside. Make sure

you tie them good, 'cause if you don't, you're going to be in trouble! Tell the rest of the boys to start herding those cattle to the nearest town and sell them quick!"

Fred and Barney were made to get off their horses while Big Jake watched, grinning. Barney tried to sneak the book under his shirt hoping the thieves wouldn't see it, but Big Jake spotted him and grabbed the book away.

"What's this?" he asked, turning the pages.

"It's nothing important," said Fred, hurriedly. "Give it back to us. You wouldn't be interested in it."

"I wouldn't, huh? Well, if it isn't important, why did you two guys bring it with you and why are you so worried about it? I think I'll just

take it and look through it very carefully. Who can tell what I'll find."

"Now we're **really** in trouble, Barney," whispered Fred, as they were taken to the hillside hideout. "We're out in the middle of nowhere and now we've lost the only means of getting home!"

Big Jake watched as Bill tied Fred's and Barney's hands. Then he took them inside the hideout and sat them down in a corner.

The inside of the hideout looked just like a house. The hill had been hollowed out very carefully and then the walls had been strengthened with wood and stone. There were bunks for sleeping and a stove for cooking. There was even a desk and a chair. Big Jake checked

Bill's handiwork on the bonds and then he sat down at the desk and looked at Fred and Barney with cruel amusement.

"No one will ever find you here," he said. "The law has been looking for us for a long time but they haven't got a clue as to where we go after we steal the cattle." Leaning back in the chair, he propped his feet on the desk and continued. "We can't let you go. You know our secret. So I've got a little proposition for you. If you join us, we'll cut you in for a regular share, just like the other guys. If you say no, well, we'll just have to arrange a little accident for you. Those things happen to people all the time out here. I'm going to give you

some time to think about it while I read your book. I hope you make the right decision." Laughing, Big Jake opened the book and started to read to himself. A short time later, however, Fred and Barney could see his eyes beginning to droop. Presently, Big Jake was asleep with the book resting on his chest.

"Now's our chance to try to escape, Barney," whispered Fred. "That outlaw, the one Big Jake called Bill, didn't tie my hands very well, because I tightened my muscles without his knowing it. Now my ropes are loose. If I work at them, I think I can slip them off."

"Hurry up, " said Barney. "I don't know how long Big Jake will stay asleep."

Fred worked hard at the ropes for a few minutes and was rewarded when they loosened enough for him to slip his hands through. He leaned over and quickly untied Barney, as well. Now the only problem was how to get the book back without waking Big Jake.

"This is going to take a delicate touch," Fred whispered to Barney. "Your hands are smaller than mine. You try it."

Barney walked across the floor of the hideout on tiptoes. When he reached Big Jake's side, he carefully stretched out his hand to grasp the book. The outlaw did not stir. Barney's nimble fingers snatched the book very carefully from Big Jake's chest.

Then, he and Fred made their way over to the door and slipped out.

Outside, they saw that their horses were tied up with the horses of the cattle thieves. Some of the men were standing near by.

"This calls for the triumph of brains over brawn," said Fred. "Let me handle this."

Squaring his shoulders, Fred walked confidently over to the men.

"Big Jake has convinced us to join your gang," he said. "He is taking a nap right now, but he told us to go and help you men. I guess you'd better give us our horses."

The outlaws looked at Fred and Barney suspiciously, but Fred

kept up his air of authority and finally, they shrugged their shoulders and untied the horses. The reins of Fred's horse's bridle had been fixed and he thanked the men as he and Barney mounted and prepared to ride away.

Suddenly, the door of the hideout burst open and Big Jake came running out shaking his fist.

"Catch them, you fools," he shouted!

Fred and Barney kicked their horses into a gallop and rode away as fast as they could. Behind them, they heard shouts and when they turned to look, they saw the cattle thieves riding after them.

"I'd better check the book," said Barney, and he opened it.

"Hurry up, Barney," cried Fred. "We can't go on like this much longer!"

"I'm doing the best I can," said Barney. "Reading and riding don't mix! It says here on page one hundred and ninety-seven that the two brave cowboys knew they were in trouble because their horses were tiring . . . . . ."

"That's not important," shouted Fred. "Read **ahead** and see what happens next!"

"It says, 'Just when things appeared darkest for the brave cowboys, they looked up to see a posse riding toward them.'"

"And there they are," Fred cried, pointing.

To their relief and amazement, Fred and Barney saw Jim and Cookie riding swiftly toward them,

followed by several other men wearing stars on their jackets. The thieves had spotted the riders as well, for behind them, Fred and Barney heard their shouts of fear and dismay. Turning in their saddles, they saw the thieves turn hastily and ride back toward the hideout. Jim and Cookie caught up with them a few seconds later, while the posse rode past, pursuing the outlaws.

"We've been looking all over for you," Jim shouted. We brought the law with us this time, but if we hadn't heard the noise you guys were making, we never would have found you or the thieves. We owe you a debt of thanks for leading us to them."

"It was nothing," Fred said modestly.

"Hey, Fred," said Barney. "It says right here, on page two hundred and twelve that the two cowboys rode off into the sunset. Then it says 'The End'. We've come to the end of the book."

"Yabba dabba doo," shouted Fred. "We're going home!"

Fred and Barney turned their horses toward the setting sun and, waving good-bye to their bewildered friends, they began riding into the desert.

Suddenly, everything became blurry and the scenery in front of them began to waver.

"It's working," cried Barney.

In the blink of an eye, Fred and Barney found themselves back in the library, the horses gone.

"Put that book back in the shelf and let's get out of here," yelled Fred. He grabbed for the knob of

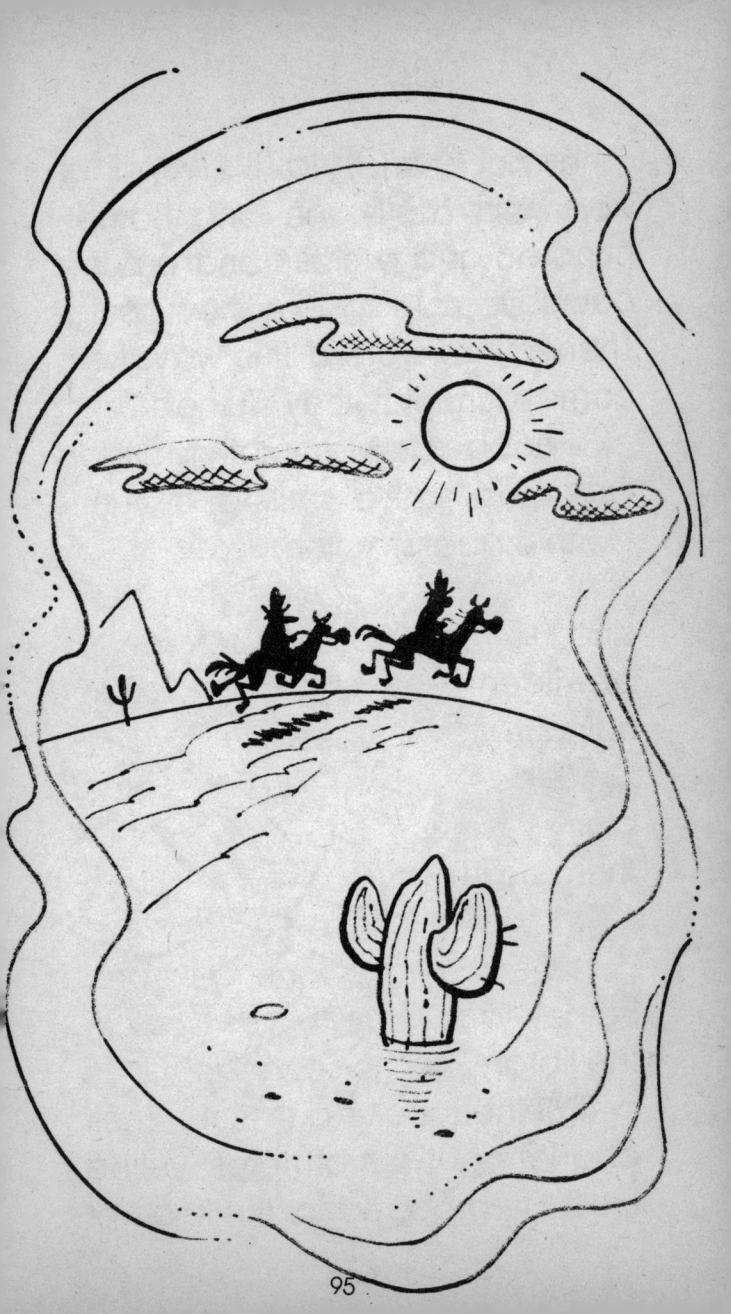

the door and, to his relief, it opened easily. He and Barney ran down the stairs and out the front door as fast as they could. When they were a little ways from the mansion, they turned and looked back. Mammoth Mansion seemed to be smiling at them with evil satisfaction.